# MY LOVE FOR YOU All Year Round

## Susan L. Roth

Dial Books for Young Readers  New York

Published by Dial Books for Young Readers
A division of Penguin Young Readers Group
345 Hudson Street
New York, New York 10014

Copyright © 2003 by Susan L. Roth
All rights reserved
Manufactured in China on acid-free paper
Designed by Kimi Weart
Text set in Martin Gothic

1 3 5 7 9 10 8 6 4 2

To make these collages, I used big and small scissors,
curved and straight tweezers, Japanese rice-based paste,
and papers from everywhere.

Library of Congress Cataloging-in-Publication Data
Roth, Susan L.
My love for you all year round / Susan L. Roth.
p. cm.
Summary: Two mice describe their love in terms of the special
characteristics of each month of the year.
ISBN 0-8037-2796-8
[1. Love—Fiction. 2. Months—Fiction. 3. Year—Fiction.
4. Mice—Fiction.] I. Title.
PZ7.R737 Myf 2003
[E]—dc21   2002001631

Thank you:
as ever, JR, AAA, M; prototype: Cindy Kane;
collaboration: Karen Riskin, Kimi Weart, Lily Malcom;
handmade papers: Michael Laufer; calligraphy: Sheila Swan Laufer;
garden: Joe Calisi; river.

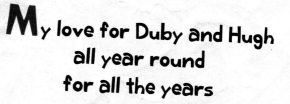

My love for Duby and Hugh
all year round
for all the years

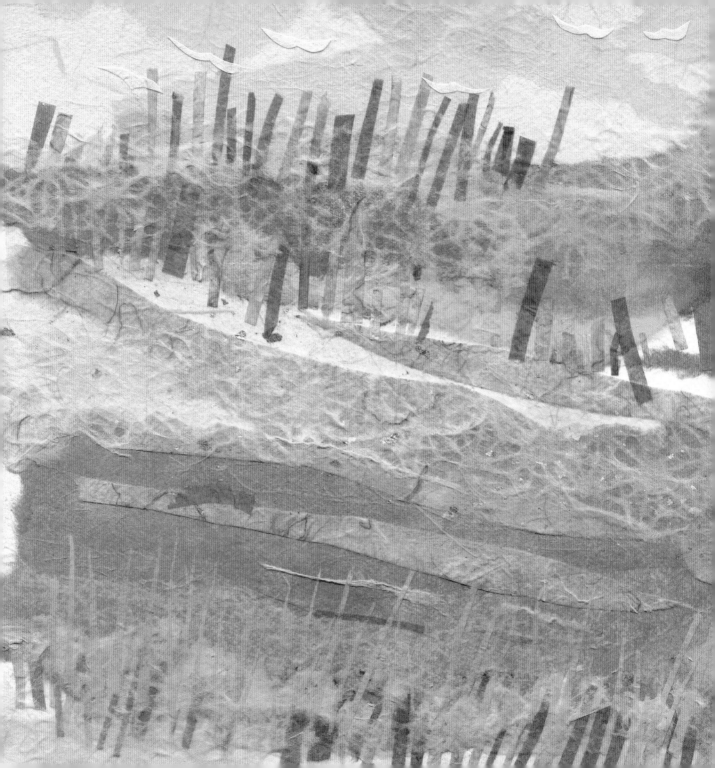

My love for you . . .

is warmer

than a snowsuit

in JANUARY,

sweeter than heart-shaped chocolates

in FEBRUARY,

My love for you
all year round

gentler than

a newborn lamb

in MARCH.

My love for you . . .

is softer than APRIL rains,

brighter than MAY wildflowers,

sunnier than

the longest day

in JUNE.

My love for you . . .

is louder than fireworks in JULY

and quieter than

a lazy AUGUST afternoon.

My love for you . . .

is rosier than

a SEPTEMBER apple,

plumper than

an OCTOBER pumpkin,

fuller than families in NOVEMBER,

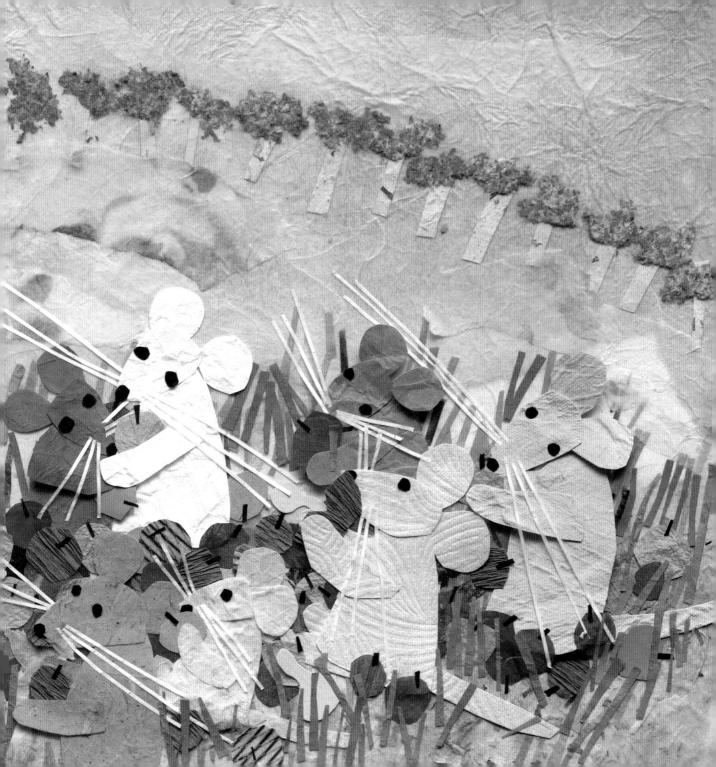

cozier than

a hundred holiday hugs

in DECEMBER.

My love for you is

softer

sweeter

warmer

brighter

gentler

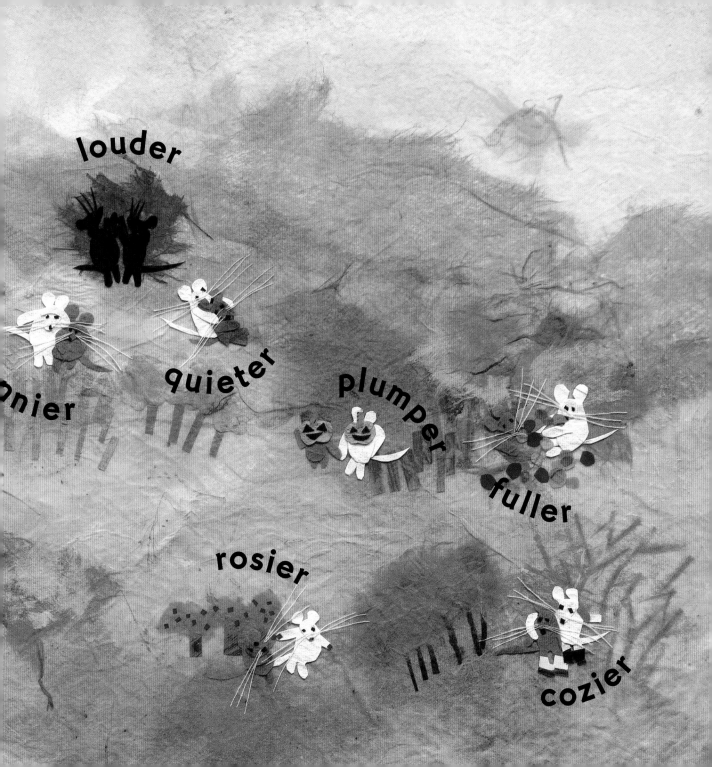

all year round.